# A Way with
# Wild Things

**Larissa
Theule**

**Sara
Palacios**

Poppy Ann Fields liked bugs.
They were her friends.

She sat among the wildflowers, listening patiently
to the sounds of nature all around her.

She coaxed the shy roly-poly out of her shell.

When the ants marched over her, Poppy let them,
even though she was ticklish.

She recognised the spider mama's weaving
for what it was – magnificent art.

And she spent long afternoons talking with the ladybirds
about shapes and colours and the heights of flowers.

But when she was around **people**, Poppy felt shy
and preferred to disappear into the background.

At parties she hid in stripes . . .

. . . and in big bright **florals**.

She became a **landscape**...

or a **tree**.

She was the **pouring** rain,

a **patterned** curtain,

a **leopard** in a menagerie.

When Grandma Phyllis turned 100,
Poppy stood watching the party from a distance.

Guests milled about, coming together
to **hug** and shake hands.

Some people **danced**. Children **ran**.

They looked like colourful leaves
**falling** into each other then **drifting** apart.

A small wind blew across the garden. On it rode a **dragonfly**. He landed on the cake. How his wings *shimmered* in the sun!

Poppy **clapped** her hands, filled with delight.

Uncle Dan said, "Poppy Ann Fields, *there* you are!"
His voice was louder than the humming
of a **thousand** dragonflies.

The guests went quiet.
Poppy froze.
Every eye fell upon her.
She felt her cheeks go **red**.

The dragonfly *flew* off the cake . . .

. . . and landed in her hand.

Someone gasped.
"Did you see that?"
"It flew to her like it knows her."

"Poppy's got a way with wild things,"
said Grandma Phyllis.

Everyone came in for a closer look.

Poppy's feet **refused to move.**

She would have liked to run
to the trees beyond the garden.
She wished the people would all
turn away and leave her alone.

She couldn't look at them,
so she looked at the **dragonfly,**
soft and fragile in her hands.

She knew the dragonfly had come here for her.

The wind *lifted* her hair, cooled her face.

The wildflowers *swayed* beneath the trees.

She **breathed**.

"What a **beautiful** dragonfly!"
said one of the guests.

"The scientific name is *Anisoptera*,"
said Poppy softly, but clearly.

"You wildflower, you," whispered Grandma Phyllis.

The small wind still blew.

Poppy knew she didn't have to disappear into the background.

Leaves and wings *fluttered* to the beat of her heart.

She was bright and full of colour . . .

. . . just like a **wildflower**.

For Anya, my wildflower
L.T.

To my husband, Ed, for not
letting me blend in with
the background anymore
S.P.

BLOOMSBURY CHILDREN'S BOOKS Bloomsbury Publishing Plc
50 Bedford Square, London WC1B 3DP, UK

BLOOMSBURY, BLOOMSBURY CHILDREN'S BOOKS and the Diana logo
are trademarks of Bloomsbury Publishing Plc

First published in Great Britain in March 2021 by Bloomsbury Publishing Plc

First published in the USA in March 2020 by Bloomsbury Children's Books
1385 Broadway, New York, New York 10018

Text copyright © Larissa Theule, 2020
Illustrations copyright © Sara Palacios, 2020

Larissa Theule and Sara Palacios have asserted their rights under the Copyright, Designs
and Patents Act, 1988, to be identified as Author and Illustrator of this work

ISBN 978-1-5266-2856-5

2 4 6 8 10 9 7 5 3 1

Printed and bound in China by Leo Paper Products, Heshan, Guangdong

All papers used by Bloomsbury Publishing Plc are natural, recyclable products from
wood grown in well-managed forests. The manufacturing processes conform
to the environmental regulations of the country of origin

To find out more about our authors and books visit www.bloomsbury.com
and sign up for our newsletters